Just Right for Two

For Finlay and Dylan, with love
T. C. xx

For my darling Iris
R. B.

First U.S. edition 2014

Library of Congress Catalog Card Number 2013955661
ISBN 978-0-7636-7344-4

14 15 16 17 18 19 GBL 10 9 8 7 6 5 4 3 2 1

Printed in Shenzhen, Guangdong, China

This book was typeset in Bell MT.
The illustrations were done in mixed media.

Nosy Crow
An imprint of
Candlewick Press
99 Dover Street
Somerville, Massachusetts 02144

www.nosycrow.com
www.candlewick.com

Just Right for Two

Tracey Corderoy

illustrated by

Rosalind Beardshaw

nosy crow
An imprint of Candlewick Press

Dog had a big blue suitcase.

He took it with him everywhere.

Inside were all his special things . . .

a bumpy little
pinecone,

a smooth rock
with a hole in it,

some dancing
leaves,

a really
good stick,

a soft, tickly
feather,

and a big, shiny red
button.

With his special things safely
packed away, Dog watched the moon rise.
"I have everything I need!" he told the stars.
Then he snuggled down on his big blue suitcase,
which was just the right size for one.

But the next morning, when he woke up . . .

someone else was sleeping
on his big blue suitcase, too!

"Hey! You can't sleep there!" cried Dog.

"Oh! Why not?" asked Mouse.

"Because all my special things
are in there," Dog said.

"Can I have a peek inside?" asked Mouse.

"Then I'll go—I *promise*!"

"Just one tiny peek," Dog said.

"I have everything I need in here,"
he told Mouse.

Mouse admired Dog's special things.
"Thank you for showing
them to me," he said.

"Now, before I go, how about a game of hide-and-seek?"

"Just one tiny game," Dog said.

So Dog and Mouse
played one tiny game

that turned into
a big game!

Then Mouse went
on his way . . .

"That was fun," Dog said
when the game was over.

and the woods
suddenly felt quiet.

To cheer himself up,
Dog opened his suitcase

and looked at
his **special** things.
But that didn't
make him feel better.

"Something just doesn't feel
right," he said.

"Maybe *Mouse* could help!"

So Dog set off
to find him.

Luckily, Mouse was not far away.

"Oh, Dog!" cried Mouse. "You look sad.
What's wrong?"

"Well," said Dog, "I thought I had
everything I needed in my suitcase . . .

but now I think I need
something else!
What can it be?"
"Don't worry," said Mouse.
"Whatever it is, we'll find it!"

So Dog searched one way . . .

and Mouse searched the other,
both trying to find the something else
that Dog needed.

On and on and on they searched, until . . .

bump!

"It's you!" cried Dog, scooping up his friend.
"You're the special something else I need!"

"Me?" said Mouse.

"But I'm nothing special."

"You're you!" said Dog.

"And that's *very* special."

Later, when they sat down for a snack,
Mouse said, "I've had the best day ever!"

"Me too," agreed Dog.

That night, Dog and Mouse
watched the moon rise together.

They sat side by side
on the big blue suitcase, which
was **actually** just the right size . . .

for two!